The Cat

From

Another world

By Jane S. G. Kostman

Chapter 1
The Arrival to a New Town

Peter Lee Williams sat in the front passenger seat of the silver Toyota Sienna. Peter was still upset that he had to move and lose all his friends.

He held a small grudge about the move but kept silent. The radio played country music on low volume. No one was listening it was only background noise.

Mrs. Charlotte Mia Williams was happy when she got a call from her husband Jack Anthony Williams. He finally sent for them to travel to Park City, Utah their new home. Charlotte knew this was going to be a big change.

She kept telling her son Peter to think of this as a new family adventure. Peter was an only child and his parents could not have any more kids.

After having a miscarriage three years ago. Charlotte had many doctors say a partial hysterectomy was necessary. They said getting pregnant again could kill her.

They hoped they could give Peter a brother or sister but because of the danger of another pregnancy. Peter would remain an only child.Charlotte felt relieved as she saw the sign for Park City, Utah. She looked at Peter.

"Only 7 More miles and we will be arriving at our new home. Peter nodded but was not happy. He continued to look out the window. Seeing the town as they drove down the towns main street.

Park City, Utah was a small town. The highest population was around 8300. The William family came from Seattle.This was going to be a change that would take time to adjust to. The beauty of Park City, Utah was amazing to Charlotte.

The mountains were gorgeous and Salt Lake City was 32 miles away. Mr. Williams worked in Salt Lake and set his practice up there.

Park City Utah was also famous for skiing. None of the Williams knew how to ski. But now that this was their new home there was a chance they could learn.

Peter Lee Williams would attend Park City High School. Peter felt forced to finish his freshmen year, 9th grade there. He recently turned 14.

Mr. Williams was a dentist and very experienced in his field of work. He finally had his own office in Salt Lake, city. He was there three months before sending for His wife and his son.

Charlotte had always had faith in her husband to do what was good for the family. She was a kindergarten teacher for over 12 years now.

Charlotte knew she would be starting over in Park City, Utah. She would be starting in 1 week at Little Miners Montessori school. She was excited as always when it came to new adventures.

Park City, Utah was a small town. The highest population was around 8300. The William family came from Seattle.

This was really going to be a change that would take time to adjust to. Charlotte was amazed at how beautiful Park City, Utah was.

The mountains were gorgeous and Salt Lake City was 32 miles away. Mr. Williams worked in Salt Lake and set his practice up there.

Park City Utah was also famous for skiing. None of the Williams knew how to ski. But now that this was their new home there was a chance they could learn.

Peter Lee Williams would attend Park City High School. Peter was forced to finish his freshmen year, 9th grade there. He just turned 14.

Mr. Williams was a dentist and was a really good one. He finally had his own office in Salt Lake, city. He was there three months before sending for His wife and his son.

Charlotte had always had faith in her husband to do what was good for the family. She was a kindergarten teacher for over 12 years now.

She knew she would be starting over in Park City, Utah. She would be starting in 1 week at Little Miners Montessori school. She was excited as always when it came to new adventures.

Chapter 2

The Mysterious Old House

The car came to a stop and Charlotte pulled to the side. In front of them stood a faded blue house with yellow trim.

The white fence was cracked and the paint had started peeling off. The mailbox was slanted and it was missing the back and front pieces.

The grass was brown and there was toilet paper all over the yard. The metal gate to the fence was lying on the grass and looked bent and rusted.

Charlotte looked at her son in the passenger seat. She touched his shoulder softly. As he turned towards her she said,"Why don't you start unloading the car. I am going to go inside and find your dad".

·Peter grumbled. "Okay mom". They both unbuckled their seat belts. Charlotte headed towards the front door of the house. As she stood in front of the door she peered in the diamond-shaped glass that looked like it had a goldish hew. Because of all the dirt stuck around the edges.

Hello! Charlotte yelled as she grabbed the door knocker to knock. Once Charlotte grabbed the door knocker it felt to the ground and something crawled on the door. A few spiders.

Charlotte jumped back and screamed. Catching her breath! She put her hand across her chest and closed her eyes and looked up.

Peter came running over Mom! He shouted "Are you okay? I heard you scream." Yes, Peter, I am okay. I had a small scare."

She pointed towards it. Peter looked at where she pointed. He understood when he saw the small spiders.

But Peter's was also hoping to see his dad. Mom Is dad here? Peter asked.

I don't know! I knocked and there is no answer. I don't have a key yet. Your dad is supposed to meet us here. Charlotte said. Peter started looking around and he noticed several lawn ornaments on the porch.

On the first step there was a small frog, and on the second step an Owl, and on the fourth step there was a big rock. Peter looked under each of them and found a key under the frog. Mom Here is a key! Peter exclaimed.

Charlotte grabbed the key and went towards the door. The spider left so she inserted the key in the keyhole and turned the key. The door opened! Relief set in again and she started to calm down.

The house looked as if no one had lived there in years. The furniture was all covered in sheets that looked off-white. The hardwood floors were so dirty. You could tell they had not been cleaned in years, and the floors had so many cracks they looked centuries old.

Even the design in the house looked old. The wood carvings and molding of the house. Seemed much older inside the house than outside the house. The house also had a strange smell to it.

As they walked across the floor they left behind them footprints. The floor creaked and a grandfather clock in the living room chimed in a spooky way. Peter and his mom jumped. The sound of the Coo-cooing bird sounded strange. They watched it flap its wings and enter back into the clock once it was finished chiming.

The walls were painted with a faded yellow. The pictures that hung on the wall were all covered in dust. So much dust they looked almost empty. The curtains, once white looked greyish. Peter and Charlotte wondered how someone could let a house get so dirty.

The table was stacked high with books. Books of every kind. Encyclopedias, cookbooks, novels and a diary. There were many types of notebooks, romance novels, children books and many more books.

Peter grabbed a book with the title "A cat from another world". He read the title out loud to himself as he dusted the book.

He flipped through the pages of the book and the pages were blank. Strange he thought. Then he wondered why all the pages of the book was blank.

Seeing a nice pen on the table. Peter decided to write his name on the first page.

Charlotte found her way into the kitchen. The house was shining with such a dim light and the lights on the ceiling continued to flicker.

Charlotte looked around the kitchen. She saw pots that hung on metal hooks from the ceiling that looked like they had not been used in many years. The fridge was big and wide with nothing in it.

The smell in the fridge made the whole kitchen stink once the refrigerator's door opened. Charlotte gagged at the smell and covered her mouth and nose. It smelt as if there were eggs that had gone bad. Yet, there was not any food in the fridge or freezer.

Once Charlotte shut the fridge. She continued to explore the kitchen. She looked through some of the cupboards. There were 12 on one side of the kitchen 15 on the other.

And each cupboard she looked inside was empty. The color of the cupboards like the rest of the house faded in color. The cupboards looked off-white and had a yellowish color. Dishes had dust on them and the counters were cracked.

Charlotte headed to the sink and turned on the facet and wanted to see if they at least had running water. They did, yet it was brown with a smell like sewer water.

Charlotte could not help but think to herself she made a mistake coming here. She tried her husband's cell phone again, nothing. It kept going straight to voicemail. Which left her feeling frustrated.

This house was going to need a lot of work. Peter! Charlotte called. Yes, mom! Peter said as he stood in front of her. What's that? His mom asks. After seeing something in his hands.

It's a book mom, but nothing's written on its pages. Except, I did write my name in it. Charlotte looked around in the book at the blank pages. They must of faded years ago sweetheart. You should use it as a journal or write a story on its blank pages. Charlotte said.

Charlotte turned the book to the back looking for a date. There was a lot of writing on the back. Some were hard to make out. But inscribed was a warning. Don't read out loud!

She found a date on the back of the book. Strange! Charlotte said out loud. What is it, mom? Peter asked. Well, sweetheart the date says 1901. Charlotte said.

"Hmm," Peter said. Pausing a second to think. It has to be a miss print mom! Peter said. Yeah, it would have to be! Charlotte said.

She handed the book back to him. They headed upstairs to see how the bedrooms looked. The first bedroom had faded blue walls. Almost hard to tell it had been a darker blue because it was so faded.

The furniture in the room they went in was also covered in sheets. After removing some sheets they found a dusty and dirty bed.

It had two pillows in off-white pillowcases. The top cover was also off-white with a faded design. The bed frame was metal and faded gold.

The dresser was an off brown and had old clothing in it. In the closet, there were white gowns and boxes of many things. Candles on top of the dresser.

There were even boxes and boxes of letters. Mom look at this one! Peter exclaimed. Charlotte grabbed the letter. She noticed that the writing was in calligraphy.

Opening the letter she saw most the letter had faded out. The letter was old and yellowed from age. Charlotte handled the paper very careful in hopes it wouldn't tear. She held it up to the light and still could not make out much.

Dearest Love,

Sincerely,

Ryan R. Miles

Charlotte was able to read only the dark letters.
Which read Dearest Love, Sincerely, Ryan R.
Miles. She set the letter back into the box and she
grabbed another letter. Each letter was the like
the other. Unable to read and faded.

Peter and Charlotte continued exploring the
house. In the next room, they found it to be like
the other bedroom.

Old clothing, old photos hanging on the wall, old
letters, old everything. The bed in that room was
also covered in sheets too. The whole house
reeked of dust as if no one ever had lived there.

Peter, we should do a light cleaning here. It is
going to be dark soon and it is already 6:47 pm.
Charlotte said.

But mom! Peter protested, what about Dad? Charlotte shook her head as she said I don't know! I'll try his phone again in the morning.

I am pretty tired son. I say we camp out downstairs by the fireplace. Charlotte said. What about all the dust mom? Peter said in protest. We will clean the best we can. Charlotte said.

Peter shrugged. He knew this was a battle he could not win.

Suddenly out of nowhere, there was a loud crash coming from downstairs. Peter shrieked. Mom! Mom! There is someone in the house. What do we do? Peter said in a low tone as he was frightened.

Maybe it's your father. Charlotte said. As she turned to open the bedroom door.

Peter jumped in front of her. Mom! This is how horror movies start! Charlotte rolled her eyes and tried for the door again.

Mom wait! Peter ran towards the closet he grabbed a metal bat. It was heavy and old. What are you doing with that Peter? It's for protection.

Oh, give me a break peter! Charlotte said. Mom this house is very strange. And we don't know who is down there. You have been trying to get ahold of Dad for a couple days now.

You think by now dad would have called! Peter said in a scared but brave tone. Charlotte thought about it and then said, "Your right!" Although, I am sure we have nothing to worry about. She embraced her son for a short hug.

Mom, get behind me! The door creaked as they headed downstairs. The stairs also creaked. Peter looked back at his mom. Sorry! She said in haste.

The stairs Charlotte stepped on creaked louder than when he stepped on it. The living room was darker than before. Peter asked his mom for her phone. He turned on the flashlight.

He held the bat tight in one hand and the phone in the other. Looking around they saw there were books on the floor knocked down from the table. As they turned with a scare they had heard a creek in the kitchen and a loud bang.

Charlotte was going to head that way but Peter held her back. Mom! We should run! Let's get outta here!

Charlotte was hesitant and unsure what to do. Then they heard another loud crash from upstairs and what sounded like footsteps. Mom! Let's go! Peter cried! Charlotte said we can't go I don't have my car keys or purse.

Mom your keys! Peter waved them! As he continued to move towards the door! Looking at his mom and saying come on mom! Let's go! Charlotte let out a breath of relief. What about my purse! Charlotte asked. It's in the car! Peter said.

Another loud crash and what sounded like more footsteps set them running for the front door. Neither of them could run fast enough. Peter tossed the keys to his mom she unlocked the door with the push of a button.

Both got in the car as fast as they could. Leaving the front door of the house open. Charlotte started the car and drove off. Buckle up! Charlotte demanded.

As they drove away the lights went on and off in the house. The bedroom lights flickered and the living room lights went on and off and the door slammed shut.

Mom! Did you see that Peter exclaimed! Charlotte could drive away faster. She shook her head in disbelief. Mom! Peter yelled. Yes, Peter, I saw that! I don't know if I can believe I saw that! Can we not talk about it right now Peter? Charlotte said.

Peter shook his head in agreement. Out of the blue, they heard a meow that made them jump. Peter looked back and saw a cat black and grey as night with bright green eyes that had yellow hew. Mom, We have a stowaway. Peter exclaimed grabbing the cat.

Can we keep him? Peter begged. Peter that cat doesn't belong to us. He might have a home. Charlotte said. Okay, mom, I will make all the flyers for him and put them up around town on one condition.

Charlotte looked at her son and then back at the road. Peter held the Cat he looked so beautiful and he was meowing a lot.

What's the condition? Charlotte asked. I get to keep him if no one claims him. Charlotte said we will see. Peter continued to pet the cat. I am going to call you Midnight.

Meow! The cat said looking into Peter's eyes almost with a protest. You like midnight don't you? Meow. The cat said. Peter grinned as he continued to pet the cat.

Chapter 3

The Hotel and the cat

Charlotte drove to a hotel and they got a room for the night. Then they ordered a pizza. Charlotte tried her husband's cell phone again. She was in disbelief that there was still no word from her husband and still no answer.

She was feeling pretty disappointed. Anything from dad? Peter asked.

Charlotte shook her head as she sat next to her son in the bed. Trying to be strong she said to Peter. Dad could be busy working.

Mom! Peter said. Dad never does anything like this. We should put out a missing person report mom. Peter said. Not yet, I am sure your father is fine Peter. Charlotte said .

But Mom Dad always calls at least once a day. Peter said. This made Charlotte feel worse. I think something happened to him. Peter said.

Charlotte changed the conversation, Well, get some sleep we have a busy day tomorrow.

Where is the cat? Charlotte asked and as soon as she did the cat jumped on the bed. The cat sat at the foot of the bed almost in protest.

He had a strange looking collar with a ball around it that was glass and on the side to other glass balls.

The collar on the cat's neck had several sparkles in it and looked old. It was a little bigger than the size of a quarter. His bright green eyes glared at them as if to tell them something.

The cat meowed and meowed. I hope he doesn't meow all night. Charlotte said. Peter got comfortable and so did Charlotte. They hit the lights at 9:30 pm. The hotel was quiet and they both rested good until 7 am. The cat woke Peter by sitting on his chest.

Get up! Get up! The cat said while batting at peters face with his paw.

Peter slowly opened his eyes. The cat glared at him as he said Get up! Peter started to freak out.

You -you! Yes, I speak! The cat said. Lest your not deaf! You sure did not get the hint last night. The cat said.

Now get up! The cat demanded. Peter slapped himself in the face this is a bad dream and any minute I will wake up.

If you don't get up your father won't be the only one in danger. The cat said very loud.

In danger? Peter questioned. Must you repeat everything I say? The cat said in anger. Sorry! I am not used to talking to a cat! Peter said.

Now about your father, the house has him hostage. Well, not only the house but those who used to live in the house. The cat said. "How can a house..?" Peter began but the cat interrupted him? Enough questions. We have to go. Now! The cat yelled in a demanding way.

What about my mom? Leave her here. She will only get you into more danger. If I leave her she will be so mad. Peter said.

"Fine bring her but make it fast. We are running out of time." The cat said.

Mom! Mom! Peter yelled as he shook her. Allow me. The cat said. As he jumped on the bed and yelled GET UP NOW! Your husband is in danger, and you will be too if you don't do as I say.

Charlotte sat up in bed pretty fast. He -He is a talking cat! She said a little freaked out and then screamed. The cat slapped her with his paw. Do you have to scream? The cat said.

Do you know how much it hurts my ears? You humans never change. You seem to scream and freak out about everything. The cat said. As he slapped her one more time. I am not sure if I made myself clear. GET UP! The cat said in a loud voice.

Mom! Come on! There is no time the cat is going to explain on the way! We have to go! Dad is trapped in the house! Charlotte and her son Peter and the Cat headed to the car.

The cat explained what he could to them as they started to drive in the direction of that creepy house. The house is not a house. It's a decoy ship. A ship? Peter and Charlotte asked out loud.

Here we go with the repeating thing. The cat said sarcastically. Yes, it is a ship from my world. Don't you listen? The cat said. Sorry, Peter said. You were saying. The house- or ship whatever you want to call it. Was shapeshifted into a house in 1901 but the rulers of my world.

Like the empty book? Peter asked.

You know it's not nice to interrupt. The cat yelled. Sorry. Peter said again. Now where was I... the cat began. Oh yes, It's not really an empty book! The cat said in a firm voice. Well, I hope you don't get mad. I wrote my name in it. Peter said.

Why would you do that? The cat yelled. Show me the book. Now! The cat demanded.

He opened the book and the book had started to form a story. It wrote about Charlotte and Peter at the house and the hotel. The book was now alive.

Peter read on page 21 out loud," The car Charlotte drove swerved and missed a deer in the road. Then the cat knocked the book Peter read out loud down to the floor, and sat upon it."

The Cat glared at Peter and knocked the book out of his hands. Never read from this book. Do you understand? The cat said in anger.

Yes. You don't have to be so mean. Peter said in a low tone. There will be more danger! Charlotte swerved and missed a deer in the road.

Charlotte slammed on the breaks took a deep breath. Oh my Gosh, what happened! Charlotte yelled in a panicked voice.

This book is from my world! Anything read from it will happen, good or bad! This book starts out empty to the human eye like the old letters you found in the closet.

Which you should have never opened. The cat stated with a light growl. Why? Peter asked.

You don't understand. You gave the house the same key your father did. He read the empty book cover out loud like you and the letter. It brought the house into control. It has awakened the monsters inside. And brought this book back to life! It will find you!

What do you mean? Charlotte asked. Many decades ago this ship had been for the evil in my world. The people who rule my world expanded it to imprison the worst criminals in the galaxy. That house is where we stored these criminals. So it was like a prison? Charlotte asked. Yes. The cat said.

Not only a prison but an execution chamber below. Where your father is. The cat said. Does that mean dad has already been executed? Peter asked. I don't know said the cat.

How is it we understand you? Is it because of the book? Charlotte asked. In my world, we are fluent in many languages from around your world. And languages you have never heard of from my world. The cat said.

We are actually pretty intelligent and of higher intelligence, I like to think! Seriously? Peter asked. I don't know about you but cats here on earth bathe themselves with their tongues.

Lest we know how to clean ourselves ! Unlike you humans wasting away in gallons of water! The cat said.

Peter shrugged. Reaching to pet Newt. What do you think you are doing? I was going to pet you. It's one of the ways we show love to our pets. Well, Peter, I am not your pet and I never will be.

 Also, in my world, it's disrespectful to wipe your hands on another. So if you don't mind keeping your hands to yourself. The Cat said. Peter said okay.

Charlotte rolled her eyes. So Newt you are fluent in languages and for some reason, we can understand you. So why us?

Because you were in danger and close to the same fate as your husband? And your father? Really, you should be thanking me. The cat said. How do we know you are not tricking us? Charlotte asked.

I guess you will have to trust me. The cat said.

Well, why were you here in the house? I was sent to check on things. Since your father set off a few alarms. From entering the house and from reading things that should have never been read.

I have been chosen to set things back in order and make sure the monsters stay locked up.

What happens if they are released? Peter asked. Very bad things you don't want to know! The cat said. Peter looked at his mom and both shrugged.

So what do we do now Charlotte said as they pulled up to the house? Do as I say. The cat said. And then he looked at Peter. By the way, Peter do not ever call me Midnight. You humans and your pathetic names. Why it's as insulting as fluffy or snickers! The cat said.

Okay.What do we call you Peter said?

You would not be able to pronounce my real name so call me Romeo. Charlotte and Peter laughed. Well, I have always liked the name.

You must have part of a name we can pronounce. Peter said. Okay, let me think? The cat thought and said well translated into your language my name is Newt. The cat said.

"Newt. Newt. Peter repeated than said. That's unique! Charlotte asked, Where are you from Newt? Luna. Is where I am from?

It's millions of light years across the galaxy. Wow, you make it sound like your old! Peter said. No, actually I am only 313 years old. Wow. Charlotte said. Most of us live over 1200 hundred years. I am still very young. The cat said.

Chapter 4

Trapped inside

It was 10 am now and the sun shined down bright. Charlotte and Peter followed the cat back to the house.

The front steps had some type of greenish yellow slime on them. Looking across the lawn the green slime headed down towards the road.

The cat yelled it's already begun. Some of the monsters have escaped. The cat murmured in a panic!

What do we do? Peter asked as did Charlotte.

I have to get to my ship to warn my commander and they will send back up.

Where is your ship? The cat pointed toward the mountain. How do we get there?

You drive and leave the rest to me. The cat said. Charlotte, Peter, and Newt got in the car.

Charlotte started the car and they drove off. I will have to stop for gas Charlotte said. No need! The cat said.

The cat jumped into the front seat and pressed upon the dash. Light from his paw lite up the car.

Then the gas gage went from close to the E to a full tank.

Halfway up toward the mountains, the car came to a stall.

The rocky trail flattened a tire. The cat said we walk from here.

Peter and Charlotte were exhausted after walking uphill and on such a rough trail.

It felt like hours but was only 40 minutes.

Can we stop and rest Charlotte asked while breathing loudly and deeply? We are almost there? The cat said.

Looking around they spotted a cliff about 100 feet away.

The cat yelled there it is. Peter and Charlotte kept walking and arrived within 15 minutes.

Chapter 5

The Ship

Around the cliff on the bottom edge there looked to be a tiny toy ship hiding in the bushes. This is your ship? Peter asked. Yes. The cat said. That looks like a toy! Charlotte exclaimed.

Calm down! The cat yelled. I just have to enlarge it. It automatically shrinks when in a new world. It is a defense mechanism built within for safety.

Now both of you need to backup or you will be squashed. The cat said. He pressed a button on the ship and as it started to grow it took down 10 trees. Charlotte and Peter dashed under the cliff.

Alright, Come on! The cat yelled as the ship was in full form. It was the size of a football field. Why is it so big? Peter and Charlotte asked.

The cat ignored their questions. Follow me! The cat yelled. The ship was blinking with lights down a long hallway. It almost reminded Peter and Charlotte of a Sci-fi movie or star trek.

The lights turned on as they entered the ship and the ships door closed behind them. There were many automatic doors shaped in a circle that opened down the middle.

Inside the ship there were many other creatures. He yelled at one lizard looking creature an said show them to their quarters. The cat said in a loud voice.

Wait! Our quarters? They both asked at the same time.

Why is it you always repeat me? Do you know how annoying that is? The cat yelled as he sat in a nice fluffy chair and two creatures that look like small lizards waved feather on him.

Glaring at them he said listen carefully I hate to repeat myself.

You will be shown to your new living quarters! The cat said louder again. I am not living in a ship from another world. Peter yelled.

You're under my command! The cat said dont make me angry! No, newt! We are not going with you to your world. Peter said in a loud voice.

You have no choice! You are both responsible for letting those monsters out. You will meet the rulers of my world and be punished. You will be lucky to get a light punishment. Let's hope your world is not destroyed.

And when I say rulers of my world. That's me! I am the ruler of my world. I also have the power to destroy you all. With a click of a button. The cat said.

So you tricked us when we trusted you. Charlotte said.

You humans are so gullible and you believe anything. The cat said as he laughed. It was so easy to get you here. The cat laughed more. Then said, Well only few can make me laugh so I will let you live for now. Unlike your father who is already DEAD! The cat said in anger.

How do you know my dad is dead? Peter asked. Look around you, Peter. Evil creatures, in an evil world. The cat said with a evil giggle as he opened the arm of his chair and pushed a button. Bye Bye. The cat said.

The floor opened and Charlotte and Peter fell in. They fell onto a pile of garbage. Eww! Charlotte yelled! Mom, don't move! Peter said softly.

Something was moving in the trash they landed on. Suddenly out popped a cute little creature. He had 4 eyes two on the left and two on the right.

He was able to change colors. His squeak echoed in the large trash bin they happened to be in. Peter reached forward to pet the creature. The creature squeaked and licked him.

A few moments later about 50 more came out. They were friendly they had tails that were six inches long. Slender bodies and were only about two feet tall And three inches wide. Their neck was about three inches.

Mom, they are so cute. Peter said as they climbed all over him, and a few licked his ears. The first one sat on his shoulder. Charlotte had one that licked her face and hid in her long hair behind her neck.

We have got to find a way out of here! Peter said. Looking around the room there were several doors. Outside the doors were several

Chapter 6

Journey To Another World

Peter and Charlotte rolled to the other side of the ship as they felt it take off. Peter and Charlotte couldn't believe it. The cat they thought was nice turned on them. Mom, I think the ship is moving. Peter exclaimed!

Peter looked for a window. Mom, there is a window over here! It's very dirty. Peter looked for something to wipe it off. Unable to find anything he took off his shirt ripped a small piece off and put his shirt back on. Spitting on the small piece of the shirt he had taken off, he rubbed it on the window.

Mom! Look. Peter said. Charlotte looked out the window. They were in outer space for sure. She saw earth but it was far away. As they looked out the window it kept getting farther away.

How are we going to get home? Peter asked. We will find a way, Peter. Charlotte said. Then one of the creatures on his shoulder squeaked almost to understand him.

The creature jumped down and ran towards a door. It was a small door. But it opened. Peter, I can't fit in that! You will have to go! Charlotte said.

Peter squeaked in and told his mom he would be back as soon as he can. The door brought Peter to the door outside the trash room.

There was a blue box with multi-colored letters on it. Almost looked like roman numbers. Below it was a red button. Peter thought to himself. If he pushed the wrong button he was sure it would set an alarm off.

Peter stood in front of the door. Unable to decide what to press. When one of the creatures who had befriended Peter and his mom. Climbed up his leg and squeaked. As he pushed the buttons with his tiny creature fingers.

He hit about 8 different numbers than the red button and the door opened. Peter said Thank you! As he pets the creature on its head. Mom lets go! Peter yelled. His mom had not been happier seeing him.

Suddenly, there was trouble behind them. Down the hall about 30 paces. They saw lizard-like creatures with giant weapons.

The had scales on their head and wore some strange uniform that matched the color of their skin. The stood up like humans and marched in sequence stopping at the command of another lizard. Who was giving them many orders.

Peter and Charlotte hid between another hallway. They tried to stay silent and tried to hear what these lizard looking creatures were up to.

"Your leader Newt ordered destruction of earth." One lizard said. "Leave no one alive." Another said.

They continued talking but the rest was hard to make out. The lizard looking creatures. Marched down another hall. There had to be at least 200 hundred of them.

Peter and Charlotte realized right then. Newt had to of been lying to them the whole time. But how were they going to escape?

The cute creatures that squeaked alot led Peter and Charlotte to an escape pod. It was the shape of an egg and seated two.

Charlotte and Peter with a few of the creatures got in the pod. The creature pressed buttons and pointed to the steering wheel. It was circular shaped and had to be to be rolled in the direction they wanted to go.

Peter rolled the circle ball forward and they went at such a high speed. It was so fast that one of the tiny creatures bounced on the dash. The little creature was okay and just shook it off.

He jumped into Peters lap and helped him to steer. Peter and Charlotte were happy they made a few new friends. The creatures seemed to like to lick. It was almost as if it was their way of showing they like you. Charlotte had one that really liked her hair. There were about seven creatures that went with them on the ship.

Peter saw the earth and awoke his mom. Mom!
We are almost home. Peter said. Charlotte fell
asleep for about twenty minutes. Slowly they
arrived back in Park City, Utah.

Chapter 7

Return to earth

About a mile from the house the ship landed in a
big empty parking lot. The egg-like escape pod
opened from the top and folded backward. After
they got out of the pod the pod headed back
towards space.

The creatures and Charlotte and Peter started
walking back to the house. They were both

worried about Newt catching up to them.
Especially when he found out they escaped.

The front of the house looked more faded than
before. Peter and Charlotte walked into the front
door. The door slammed behind them and Locked.

"We've been waiting for you". Something in the
house echoed. Making Peter and Charlotte Jump.

"Who are you? and "Wheres my father?" Peter
yelled. As they both looked around looking for
someone.

The voice echoed back. "Your father is not with us
Newt has him."Newt. Peter said out loud. He was
angry that he ever trusted that stupid talking cat.

We were told he was dead! Peter yelled. That's not
true! The voice said."We can help you retrieve him
on one condition." Another voice said. Peter and
Charlotte looked at each other.

You have promise you are going to listen to what
we say! The voice echoed again.

Confused Peter said Newt said evil creatures were
locked up in here. He said it was like a prison for
the evil in his world.

The voice laughed. Newt is the evil in his world.
He has not been completely honest with you. The
said.

Peter and Charlotte stood in the living room still looking around. What about the book? Peter and Charlotte asked. The book is a magic book. It brings to life anything imagined by who controls it. The voice said.

Do you have the book? The voice asked. It's in my van! Charlotte said.

We took him to his ship in the van. The book with the title "The cat from another world", he told us never read from it again. Peter said.

Suddenly a door opened from upstairs. We are coming out now. The voice said. Creatures that looked like dogs of all kinds came forward. One that looked like a golden retriever came and sat in front of Peter and Charlotte.

My name is Kay. Behind me are my comrades. Introduce yourselves Kay said. A small poodle said my name is DeL. A black lab said my name is Tee. A German shepherd dog next to him said I am Gil.

A Pomeranian dog said my name is La La. All sat up so proper and were so well groomed. Each of them had the same type of collar that Newt wore.

Newt has been trying to run the galaxy for decades. He takes over planets and destroys them. He took over our home. The dog said. This is all we have left.

We understand about your dad. Del said. But newt will not give up your dad willingly. Kay said.

Newt said this was a shapeshifting house that was a ship. Kay and the other dogs laughed. Son, it would behoove you to forget everything Newt said. Gil said. Yes, it would behoove you. Tee repeated with a giggle.

Newt is halfway across the galaxy by now. Peter said. Since you escaped he may be on the way back. Kay said. Which brings me to ask how you escaped? Kay asked.

We had help. Peter said. Pointing to one of the creatures on his shoulder. What was that slime we saw on the front porch. Charlotte asked.

"Newt".Kay and his comrades said at the same time.

Son, if you have not figured it out by now, Newt is very evil. Kay said.Peter nodded.

Now I am telling both of you right now. You have to do what we say! Kay said again. They both agreed.

Chapter 8

Bringing back dad

Kay called in favor across the galaxy. They needed backup keep Newt at a distance and to protect the people of earth. Once they arrived there was a giant ship that covered the sky.

Kay directed Charlotte and Peter to the front lawn. Everything was going so fast. Peter and Charlotte and the dogs were beamed upon the ship. They were greeted by a creature that looked like a small bunny with big oval eyes and long lashes. He had extra white fur and a carrot in his left hand that he was eating a little of.

I am Bun Bun. The rabbit said and as he did with a mouth full of carrot. It splattered on Peter and Charlotte. They wiped it off onto the floor. Charlotte and Peter tried not to laugh at his name. I am the captain of this ship said Bun

Bun. Kay informed me of what's going on. Bun
Bun said."Don't you worry? I will help you get
your family back. Bun Bun said.

Did you get the book? Kay asked Bun Bun. Yes.
The book is here! He showed him a table where
the book rested. The bunny pointed to two chairs
and told Peter and Charlotte to sit in them.

Now, listen carefully. Kay said in a serious tone.
He pointed to a switch and said When I pull this
lever you both need to decide on what you want to
happen. Kay said.

What do you mean? Peter said. Imagine your
family all together. You both need to agree on
what you will imagine. So talk about that now you
have two minutes. Kay said.

Mom, can we imagine life in Seattle at our old
apartment the day before dad left to come down
here? Peter asked.

Yes, how about our family meal? Charlotte asked.
Peter smiled. Kay came over and said read from

the book. The memory you thought of Kay Said.
Bun Bun,Kay yelled.Pull the lever now. The lever
was pulled the room began to spin. And as Peter
read from the book his voice echoed.

Suddenly they were back in their apartment in
Seattle. They both were sitting at the table
laughing and eating dinner with Jack. Charlotte
winked at Peter. Both remembered their
adventure. Now they needed to convince Jack to
stay and to forget about Park City Utah.

Dad. Peter said. Yes, son Jack said. As he
continued eating. There was mashed potatoes,
green beans, and roasted chicken. Pass me the
gravy. Jack said. Peter and I were talking.
Charlotte began. We think moving is not a good
idea. Can we please stay here.? Charlotte asked.
And Peter chimed in Please!

Why the sudden change? I thought you were
happy about where we were moving and starting a
new life. Jack said.

Charlotte and Peter looked at each other. We love
Seattle to much to leave. Charlotte said and Peter
nodded his head.

Okay, we will stay here.I will call the realtor in the
morning. Jack said. You know I had the strangest

dream Jack said. Dream? Charlotte asked. Yes in the dream you both told me you didn't want to move. Jack saidSuddenly there was a knock on the door. Peter said I will get it.

Kay was sitting out front. You both forgot about Newt. You never imagined him out of the picture but don't worry we took care of that part for you. Kay said.

Where is he? Kay laughed. Floating out in space somewhere really really far away. Kay said to reassure them.

Well, I better be off. Kay said. Can't you stay?I mean I wish you could stay.Peter said.

 Stay? Kay thought. Well, I have never been a house pet? Kay said. It's easy! Peter said.

You get to go for long walks, play ball, and eat table scraps! You also get to go to the dog park, and so much more. Peter said.

Stay here I will be back. Kay took off around the corner. Peter waited for a few and was about to go in when Kay returned.

Where did you go.? Peter asked. I had to tell the others where I would be in case they need me.

 For now, I am interested in learning about being a house pet. Kay said.Peter smiled. Well do you want to go inside. Peter asked.

Yes, but you have to get my things. Kay said. Your things. Yes they are right here around the corner. kay said. Peter looked around the corner and it was a big suitcase.

He picked it up and dragged it inside. What do you have in this rocks? Peter asked. No.Kay said but you have to be careful with it. Kay said.

Peter set the suitcase down and yelled for his parents.Mom! Dad! We have a dog! Charlotte came running out of the kitchen. Kay! Charlotte said.

You guys know this dog? Jack said. Yes, we got him today! We wanted to surprise you. Charlotte said. What's the suitcase for? Jack asked. It came with the dog? Peter said. Okay. Jack said thinking it was strange.

Kay barked two times and held out his paw. Jack got down and said hey buddy. You're a smart dog! It's nice to meet you? What's his name? Jack asked. Kay both peter and Charlotte said. What a nice name. Jack said.

Kay barked in agreement. Jack smiled and pet Kay for a few and then stood back to his feet and asked why dont we finish dinner.

I am still very hungry for some reason. Jack said as he turned to Charlotte and planted a kiss on her cheek. Then they walked to the table and sat down to finish dinner.

The End

Made in the USA
Monee, IL
31 July 2022

10658249R00030